A-MAZE-ING ADVENTURES

A-MAZE-ING ADVENTURES IN NORTH AND SOUTH AMERICA

Lisa Regan

WINDMILL BOOKS

Are you ready... for the adventure of a lifetime?

Join us, Max, Millie, and our pet dog, Mojo, on a trip to see amazing and exciting sights! Everywhere we go, we will need your help. Use your finger to help us solve the tricky mazes. Along the way, we'll find hidden objects and learn some fascinating facts! We're going to take lots of photographs and make notes as we go.

Published in 2021 by Windmill Books,
an Imprint of Rosen Publishing
29 East 21st Street, New York, NY 10010

Copyright © Arcturus Holdings Ltd, 2021

Cataloging-in-Publication Data

Names: Regan, Lisa.
Title: A-maze-ing adventures in North and South America / Lisa Regan.
Description: New York : Windmill Books, 2021. | Series: A-maze-ing adventures | Includes glossary and index.
Identifiers: ISBN 9781499485493 (pbk.) | ISBN 9781499485516 (library bound) | ISBN 9781499485509 (6 pack) | ISBN 9781499485523 (ebook)
Subjects: LCSH: Maze puzzles--Juvenile literature. | North America--Juvenile literature. | South America--Juvenile literature.
Classification: LCC GV1507.M3 P484 2021 | DDC 793.73'8--dc23

All rights reserved. No part of this book may be reproduced in any form without permission in writing from the publisher, except by a reviewer.

Manufactured in the United States of America

CPSIA Compliance Information: Batch BS20WM: For Further Information contact Rosen Publishing, New York, New York at 1-800-237-9932

Find us on

Contents

Welcome to North America 4
History Trek 6
Ocean Explorers 8
The Big Apple 10
Niagara Falls 12
Dinosaur Dig 14
Welcome to South America 16
Going Deeper 18
Salty Scramble 20
Lost City 22
Rain Forest Ramble 24
Island Adventure 26
Answers 28
Glossary 30
Further Information 31
Index 32

Ted the ginger cat is going to tag along. He goes everywhere we go, but he's very shy, so he'll be hiding most of the time. See if you can find him in each maze!

Welcome to NORTH AMERICA

Huge parts of this continent are covered by Canada and the United States. We're going to start in Mexico to see its ancient sites. Then we'll head offshore to Bermuda in the Atlantic Ocean before taking a bite of the "Big Apple," New York City, where we can look down on the world from a skyscraper! Then we'll catch the spray at Niagara Falls and join a dinosaur dig in Montana.

History Trek

We are in sunny Mexico, a land full of beautiful scenery and amazing history. We are going to visit the stepped pyramids and find out more about the brilliant ancient societies that lived here.

FACT FILE

COUNTRY: Mexico
CONTINENT: North America
CAPITAL CITY: Mexico City

Mexico is a country that mixes historical sites with modern cities and tourist resorts. For many centuries, cultures such as the Toltecs, Aztecs, Maya, and Zapotecs thrived in different parts of the country. The Maya built beautiful palaces, pyramids, and temples for their rulers and gods. Ruins like those at Palenque (pictured) and Chichen Itza attract millions of visitors each year.

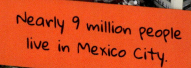

Nearly 9 million people live in Mexico City.

Ocean Explorers

Ooooh! Today we are venturing out to visit the Bermuda Triangle. It's an area full of legends and beautiful tropical fish. Let's hope we don't mysteriously vanish!

FACT FILE
COUNTRY: Bermuda
CONTINENT: North America
CAPITAL CITY: Hamilton

fishy fun

Angelfish live in the shallow waters around Bermuda.

The so-called Bermuda Triangle is a part of the Atlantic Ocean where boats and aircraft are supposed to have mysteriously disappeared. It stretches from Florida in the west, across to Puerto Rico, and up to the British islands of Bermuda. In fact, this area has no more accidents than any other busy shipping area. Bermuda itself, though, does have many shipwrecks and its own coral reefs, so it is a diver's paradise.

Watch out for the whirlpools as you navigate through the fabled waters of the Bermuda Triangle!

START

END

DID YOU SPOT?
the UFO
4 sea serpents
the periscope
the unhappy spider

The Big Apple

We are taking in the bright lights of New York City, one of the most famous cities in the world. It is a fantastic mix of people, cuisines, and cultures from all over the planet!

FACT FILE

COUNTRY: United States
CONTINENT: North America
NY STATE CAPITAL: Albany

New York City is the biggest city in the United States, and it's nicknamed the "Big Apple." It is full of famous sights, including many enormous skyscrapers that stretch high into the clouds. The highest of all is the recently built One World Trade Center. The Statue of Liberty stands at the entrance to New York Harbor and was the first thing seen by many immigrants arriving in the country to start a new life.

Catch a yellow cab to get around in the city.

Niagara Falls

There are actually three waterfalls at Niagara Falls, which sits on the border between Canada and the United States. We are excited to be in Canada, but Mojo is afraid of the water as it flows so fast.

FACT FILE

COUNTRY: Canada
CONTINENT: North America
CAPITAL CITY: Ottawa

Horseshoe Falls

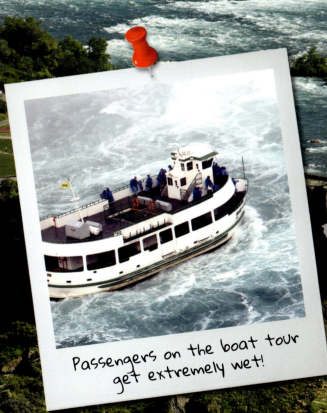

Passengers on the boat tour get extremely wet!

The largest of the waterfalls is Horseshoe Falls on the Canadian side. It is separated from the American Falls by Goat Island. The third falls, Bridal Veil Falls, is also American. The total water gushing over all three gives them the highest flow rate of any waterfall in the world. Millions of tourists visit each year. The *Maid of the Mist* boat takes you close enough to the falls to feel the spray!

Dinosaur Dig

Next on the trek is Montana, the fourth-largest state in the United States and home of Glacier National Park and the Dinosaur Trail. We're hoping to see lots of cool fossils!

FACT FILE

COUNTRY: United States
CONTINENT: North America
MONTANA STATE CAPITAL: Helena

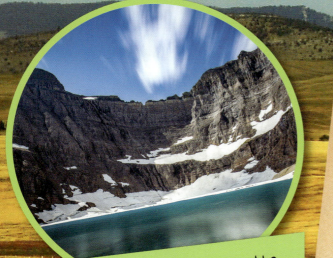

Rising temperatures make the glaciers smaller each year.

More dinosaurs have been uncovered in Montana than in any other state. There are fossils of all kinds, from the horned *Triceratops* and huge *Apatosaurus* to fierce hunters like *Deinonychus* and *T. rex*. It's a paleontologist's paradise! Glacier National Park has ancient wonders too. There have been glaciers there since an ice age 10,000 years ago.

Take a look at these dinosaur teeth!

Welcome to SOUTH AMERICA

We start our South American trek by exploring Argentina, and then we follow the mighty Andes north to Bolivia. The salt flats there are said to be amazing. We can't visit this continent without seeing Machu Picchu, high in the mountains of Peru. Then we'll trek through the Amazon Rain Forest. After all that excitement, we're heading to the Galápagos Islands for some quiet time with the animals. Phew!

Going Deeper

We have arrived in Argentina! Our first stop is at the incredible Cave of the Hands in Patagonia. It's amazing to see the paintings left by people thousands of years ago!

FACT FILE
COUNTRY: Argentina
CONTINENT: South America
CAPITAL CITY: Buenos Aires

Argentina is the eighth-largest country in the world, with a fantastic range of scenery. Patagonia is a mountainous region in the south, containing large ice fields and stunning glaciers (just visible here). The Pampas are farther north and are vast, flat grasslands where cowboys called gauchos herd cattle. The mighty Andes Mountains stretch the length of South America, from Venezuela in the north down to Argentina in the south.

The paintings in the Cave of the Hands are over 9,000 years old!

Andean condor

Check out the hand paintings at the entrance to the caves, then find your way underground to the exit.

DID YOU SPOT?

2 sets of handprints

the vampire bat

the scary monster

19

Salty Scramble

We are standing on the world's largest salt flats in Bolivia. They are absolutely vast and a brilliant, bright white!

FACT FILE

COUNTRY: Bolivia
CONTINENT: South America
CAPITAL CITY: La Paz

The landscape here is white because it is covered in a thick layer of salt, left behind when an ancient lake dried up. The valuable parts of the salt can be extracted, especially lithium, which is used in the production of electric batteries. Few living things survive out here; the main plant life is the giant cactus that grows on rocky islands on the salt flats. Flocks of flamingos gather in November to breed on the lakes nearby.

huge piles of salt

The food they eat turns flamingos pink.

Lost City

We are up in the mountains of Peru to see the magnificent Inca city of Machu Picchu. It's so amazing, it has been voted one of the new seven wonders of the world!

FACT FILE

COUNTRY: Peru
CONTINENT: South America
CAPITAL CITY: Lima

The Inca city was built high on the mountain of Machu Picchu around 1450, but when the Spanish invaded Peru in the 1500s, the city was abandoned. It was forgotten about by everyone but the locals until it was rediscovered in 1911 by an American explorer, Hiram Bingham. The site contains many houses, religious buildings, and warehouses, plus cleverly terraced fields to allow farming on the steep mountain slopes.

The Inca built temples to their sun god, Inti.

Rain Forest Ramble

We have left the bustling city behind, and now we are trekking through the Amazon Rain Forest, home to the mighty Amazon River. It's full of exciting plants and rare creatures to spot!

FACT FILE

COUNTRY: Brazil
CONTINENT: South America
CAPITAL CITY: Brasilia

The rain forest is a vast jungle that spreads across nine countries, although two-thirds of it is in Brazil. Its tropical climate makes it lush and teeming with life. The Amazon River flows through the rain forest. Although it is not the longest river in the world, it contains more water than any other river. It pours vast amounts of fresh water far out into the Atlantic Ocean.

There are 2.5 million types of insects living in the rain forest.

Island Adventure

We have left the mainland and sailed across the Pacific Ocean to the Galápagos Islands. They are tiny, but the islands are home to many amazing and unusual animals.

FACT FILE

COUNTRY: Ecuador
CONTINENT: South America
CAPITAL CITY: Quito

The Galápagos Islands are 600 miles (1,000 km) from South America, but they're part of the mainland country of Ecuador. When scientist Charles Darwin visited in 1835, he was fascinated by the creatures he found. Lots of the animals are only found on these islands, including the marine iguana, the flightless cormorant, and the Galápagos sea lion. The Galápagos giant tortoise can easily live to be over 100 years old!

Male blue-footed booby birds dance to attract a mate.

giant tortoise

Help to find a route back to the boat, saying hello to the cool creatures the gang passes on the way.

DID YOU SPOT?

the giant tortoise   the land iguana   the blue-footed booby   3 flying fish

Answers

6–7 History Trek

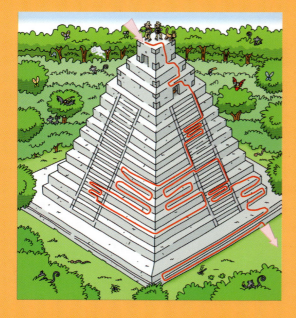

8–9 Ocean Explorers

10–11 The Big Apple

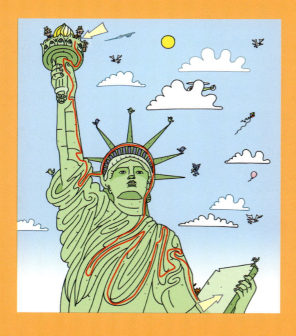

12–13 Niagara Falls

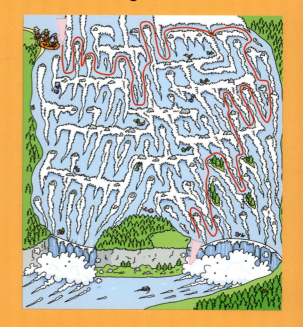

14–15 Dinosaur Dig

18–19 Going Deeper

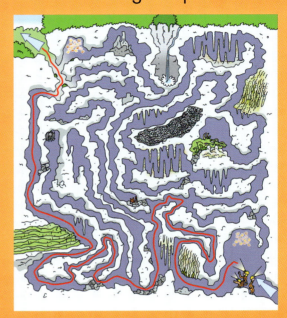

20–21 Salty Scramble

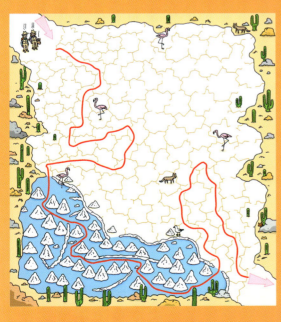

22–23 Lost City

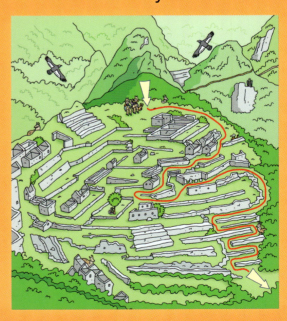

24–25 Rain Forest Ramble

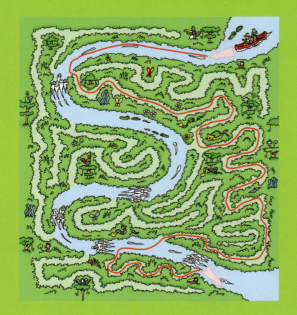

26–27 Island Adventure

Glossary

continent Any of the world's seven main landmasses.

coral reef A ridge of rock in the sea where corals have formed.

cuisine Food cooked in a particular style.

culture A group of people with particular ideas, customs, and behaviors.

fossil The remains of a prehistoric animal or plant found in rocks.

glacier A river or mass of ice that moves incredibly slowly.

immigrant A person from one country who moves permanently to live in another country.

paleontologist Someone who studies fossils and prehistoric life.

skyscraper A tall building with many stories.

Further Information

Books

Children's Picture Atlas Usborne, 2003

Mapping North America / South America (Close-Up Continents) by Paul Rockett, Franklin Watts, 2016

North America / South America (Go Exploring! Continents and Oceans) by Steffi Cavel-Clarke, BookLife Publishing, 2017

The Travel Book: A Journey Through Every Country in the World Lonely Planet Kids, 2017

Websites

www.google.com/earth

Explore the world in stunning satellite imagery.

www.natgeokids.com/za/category/discover/geography

National Geographic Kids has a wealth of information on animals and countries.

Publisher's note to educators and parents: Our editors have carefully reviewed these websites to ensure that they are suitable for students. Many websites change frequently, however, and we cannot guarantee that a site's future contents will continue to meet our high standards of quality and educational value. Be advised that students should be closely supervised whenever they access the Internet.

Index

Amazon Rain Forest 16, 24, 25
Amazon River 24, 25
Andes Mountains 16, 18
animals 8, 16, 18, 20, 24, 25, 26, 27
Argentina 16, 17, 18
Atlantic Ocean 4, 8, 24

Bermuda 4, 5, 8, 9
Bingham, Hiram 22
Bolivia 16, 17, 20, 21

Canada 4, 12, 13
continents 4, 16
coral reef 8

Darwin, Charles 26

fish 8, 9, 13, 27
fossils 14, 15

Galápagos Islands 16, 17, 26, 27
glaciers 14, 18

Machu Picchu 16, 22, 23
maps 4, 5, 16, 17
Mexico 4, 5, 6, 7
Montana, 4, 14, 15

New York City, 4, 5, 10, 11
Niagara Falls 4, 5, 12, 13

Pacific Ocean 26
Patagonia 18
Peru 16, 17, 22, 23
pyramids 6, 7

Statue of Liberty 10, 11

United States of America 4, 5, 10–15